JULIUS

By Trygve Klingsheim
Photographs by Arild Jakobsen

Yearling Nonfiction

Published by
Dell Publishing
a division of
Bantam Doubleday Dell Publishing Group, Inc.
666 Fifth Avenue
New York, New York 10103

This work was first published in hardcover in Great Britain
in 1986 by Exley Publications Ltd.

*Dedicated to Christine and Ausgunn
and, of course, Julius*

Extra photographs on pages 7, 8, 12, and 13 by Dr. William R. (Billy) Glad
Translation by Linda Sivesind
English adaptation written by Dalton Exley

Copyright © 1983 by J.W. Cappelens Forlag a.s.

ISBN: 0-440-40431-2

Reprinted by arrangement with Delacorte Press

Printed in the United States of America

April 1991

10 9 8 7 6 5 4 3 2 1

LBM

This is the true story of Julius, the chimpanzee.

Julius was born the day after Christmas, in Kristiansand Zoo, Norway. Julius was named after the Norwegian word for Christmas, which is "Jul".

Julius' father, Dennis, was a huge, twelve-year-old chimpanzee. Dennis was the "Big Boss" of the family, dominant over all the chimps.

Julius' mother was Sanne. When Julius was born she was only eight years old, a very young age for a chimp mother.

Edvard Moseid, the zoo director, and Billy Glad, the doctor, were worried about Sanne being so young. Would she be able to look after little Julius, who weighed only three pounds? Was Sanne grown up enough?

Edvard and Billy watched anxiously as tiny Julius curled up in his mother's furry arms and drank milk from her breast. Only one other baby chimp had ever been born in the zoo before, so this was both a wonderful and worrying occasion.

At first, things went well and everyone was relieved, but six weeks later, one evening in February, something terrible happened: Julius was rejected by his mother. A zoo attendant found little Julius lying alone, away from his mother. He was crying and bleeding badly. The tip of his index finger had been bitten off. Sanne, his young mother, had stopped caring for him and had left him alone and rejected.

The zookeeper hurried to telephone Edvard and Doctor Glad who rushed over to see Julius. They knew immediately that they couldn't just do nothing. Julius would die in front of their eyes, so they had to do something to help. But they both knew that if they helped Julius now and took him away from his mother and the other chimps, there would be a great danger. He might never again be accepted back by the group. Chimpanzees will not usually mix with other strange chimps, whom they often fight or even kill. Chimpanzees stay in families who all know each other and are brought up together, under one dominant leader.

So, once Julius left the chimp group for a long time they might think him a stranger if he returned, and he'd be rejected and become an outcast with no family or friends.

Edvard and Doctor Glad were in an agonizing situation deciding if they should "adopt" poor Julius. They were fully aware that Julius was a monkey and that one day he would have to go back to his own kind, where he belonged. They didn't want to adopt him and let him become a "clown to entertain human beings".

Yet it would take a long time for Julius to be old enough not to need the physical care of a "mother". It could take two years or more. Only then would he be old enough to fend for himself, and hopefully return to his chimp group.

The decision was made, Julius was to be adopted till he'd grown enough. So they wrapped Julius in a blanket and drove him to Doctor Glad's house. They gave him an anaesthetic to take away the pain and bandaged his injured finger. Doctor Glad's wife, Rodina, is a nurse so she cared for him. Julius became a patient, but instead of a hospital bed, he got a little cardboard box on the floor.

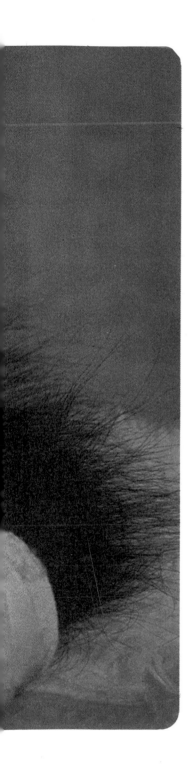

It took a long time for Julius to forget the frightening experience he'd had. When the wound healed and the bandage came off, it seemed like Julius had forgotten where he came from.

At first, Julius was adopted by Doctor Glad's family. He was full of energy, a lively monkey baby in a human family – a baby brother for twelve-year-old Carl and ten-year-old Austen.

Julius was to stay with Doctor Glad's family for a while and then live with Edvard's family. He was to keep changing homes so he would not become too attached to one family, because one day he had to go back to his real chimp family. Everyone had to try not to fall in love with cute little Julius, and this was going to be the hardest part of the whole plan.

Things were looking good; Julius drank from the baby bottle, he laughed, played and seemed happy. He even had to wear baby clothes, pampers and waterproof pants!

Julius needed a lot of love and cuddling, and he was
happiest when Edvard held him close in his arms.

After a few weeks Julius had to move back to Edvard's house. Austen gave Julius a last long cuddle and went up to his bedroom and closed the door so no one could see the tears.

Julius moved in with Edvard, Marita and their daughters, five-year-old Anne and three-year-old Siv. He moved between the two families with everyone trying not to make him decide they were his real family. This was not at all easy – caring for him, but not caring too much!

Julius was full of fun, he laughed and played with everyone. He wanted attention, tenderness and love. Julius was the focus of attention and he seemed to know it and used it to his advantage. He got furious when he wasn't allowed to do things.

Julius grew quickly – much faster than wild chimps and zoo chimps. He seemed to be behaving more like a person as each day passed, but Doctor Glad could see it was becoming important for Julius to understand he was a chimp.

One day when Julius threw his arms around Marita showering her with big kisses, tears rolled down Marita's cheeks. Anne and Siv both asked, "Why are you crying, Mommy? Can't you see Julius loves you?"

"Yes," replied Marita, drying her tears and smiling. "That's why I was crying."

Julius, who didn't understand any of the problems, jumped off Marita's lap and waddled over to the curtains. He climbed up to the ceiling and shrieked and laughed as he swung through the air. Unfortunately he overshot one clowning act and knocked his head against the wall and lost a tooth! So off to the dentist. Now, he was missing the tip of a finger and a tooth!

But soon the agile little horror was back in action. He knew where all the tasty things were kept!

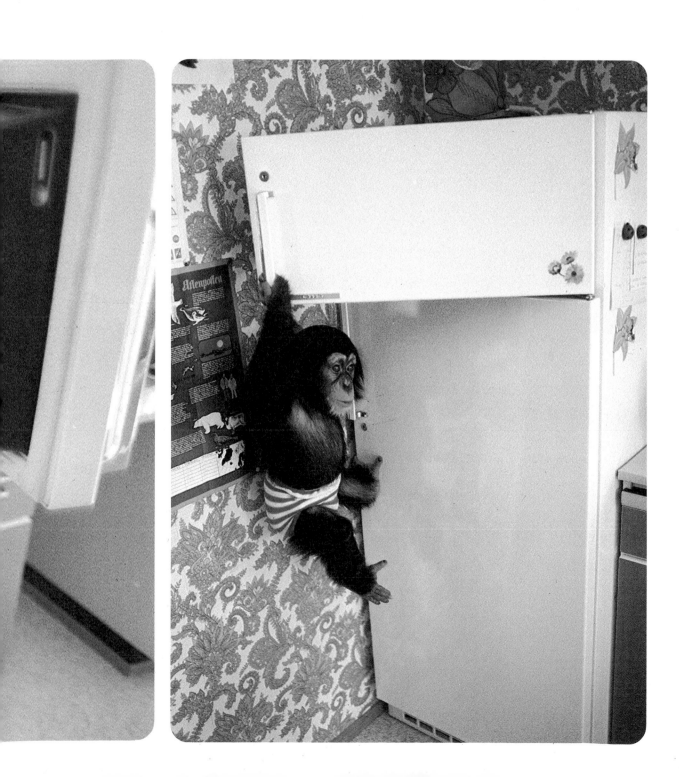

Time passed happily. Spring came with lovely sunny days. Summer arrived.

Julius burst forth with eager enthusiasm into his new world. He climbed fruit trees in the garden, went for walks in the forest with Carl and Austen. Everywhere he was discovering new things which delighted him.

He was such fun to be with – alive and full of curiosity. He wanted to know about everything he found, inquisitively looking at things and putting them in his mouth; some tasted good, others he spat out again.

Julius adored one special trip to the beach. The sand was soft and warm and made deep footprints that baffled him as they followed him! The rocks were so different and good to run on. He just had to go and taste this strange new sea. Yuk! It tasted horrible!

At Edvard's house, Julius got another treat: he had a go at painting with Anne. Julius was a born artist – the kind who delights in splodging and messing around with *all* the paints!

Julius loved it when he joined the children at bathtime. He didn't miss a trick and brushed his teeth just like the girls. When bedtime came, he would put his head under the blanket and pretend to be asleep.

Every day Julius went around with Edvard. Going to work wasn't much fun. He loved the car ride to work, but was terribly insulted because he wasn't allowed to steer!

He would go regularly to the zoo with Edvard. He was fascinated by the other animals: the bony turtle that moved so slowly and shyly hid her head inside her shell just as he tried to pet her. He just *had* to catch the rabbit so he could play with it. He was puzzled and a little nervous about the huge, but gentle, giraffe.

But when Julius saw the chimpanzees out on Monkey Island, he seemed very frightened. He clung to Edvard.

Was he afraid because he understood he was a monkey and could be rejected by them? Or did he feel like a vulnerable little person to whom the big monkeys out there on the island looked fierce and dangerous?

Perhaps he remembered the sad beginnings of his life when he was only a few weeks old? Something he wanted to forget?

Meanwhile, Edvard and Doctor Glad were worried that Julius was behaving more and more like a human every day. "It's not that he imitates us, he's learning from us," said Edvard. "But it's essential we do more so Julius understands who he is and where he belongs."

So, throughout the summer Julius was taken to the zoo every day for a few hours. From a distance he watched his real parents, Dennis and Sanne, his half brother Little Billy, and Lotta and Bølla. Julius looked over the moat at his family in an odd way, it seemed as though he thought they were strange creatures.

One of the zoo attendants rowed Julius right out to Monkey Island. Julius seemed to feel safer with the zookeeper's arm protecting him.

Julius went everywhere, even with Rodina to collect the letters. One day he saw his own picture in the paper. He couldn't work that one out.

When summer was over and the leaves fell, Julius would play with the piles of leaves that the grown-ups had carefully raked together. This was one game the grown-ups didn't appreciate very much!

The winter came. Then Christmas and Julius' first
birthday. He had a party with his own cake. Carl, Austen,
Anne and Siv were all there, but Julius was the star of the
day. He got a real treat, raspberry soda in his baby bottle.

There was an air of sadness over the kids as they wondered where Julius would be spending his next birthday ... Deep down they all knew this could be their first and last birthday party with Julius.

Winters are very cold in Norway. Julius had to stay indoors a lot, but he still saw all the strange white snow through the windows. All the trees he had climbed had changed shape and looked bare and bleak.

One day Marita rustled up some old clothes the girls had outgrown. She dressed the excitable little Julius in a warm sweater, stocking cap and snuggled him into a sheepskin baby bag.

Out in the snow Julius was mystified by this strange, new white stuff and for the first time he tasted the winter snow.

Another fresh new spring and summer came. Julius was with Edvard constantly, at work, in the zoo and even in restaurants.

He made many "people-friends," and ran around greeting everyone he met. But when he was out he never let Edvard out of his sight, and when he was scared he ran to Edvard. Usually they'd hold hands.

Julius got to know all the zoo attendants, especially Arild Jakobsen, who took the photographs for this book. Every week Arild came to see Julius and to take photos. The camera, of course, perplexed Julius. He was fascinated by everything, especially if it made strange clicks.

Julius was the zoo's most loved youngster. Everyone wanted to laugh and play with him. A T.V. special was made about him and suddenly he was known and loved by kids all over Norway.

But Doctor Glad and Edvard had to think of Julius' future
– remembering what they had decided on that February day
when he was a helpless baby, alone and close to death. During
the autumn they built a room for Julius at the zoo, right by
the room where his real chimp family lived.

There was a strong screen between the rooms so Julius and his group could all see each other, but the other chimps couldn't hurt Julius.

Julius spent many lonely hours all alone in this room, but he was visited by Doctor Glad, Rodina, Marita and the kids.

One day in autumn Edvard decided to leave Julius alone at night in his little room at the zoo. Julius slept soundly. It was Anne and Siv who had trouble sleeping – too worried about their little friend.

One day in November Edvard decided the moment had arrived to return Julius to the other chimps on the island. "They are used to seeing him, so will probably accept him now. We can't leave it any longer."

At first, Edvard took Julius out to the island and he met the hippos who shared the island with the chimps. It was scary at first, but soon Julius realized the hippos were good-natured, gentle giants.

The time had finally come for Julius to meet his family. Everyone hoped it would be all right.

Edvard let him in the room with Little Billy, his half brother, who was two months older, but much smaller than Julius. Soon the two youngsters hugged each other happily – they would be friends.

Then Julius met Bølla, the huge female chimp who was also friendly and welcoming.

Then they let Julius meet his mother, Sanne. Sadly, she again rejected her son. She didn't want anything to do with Julius even though he was her first child. She didn't hurt him again – and *that* was a great relief for everyone.

The two human families watched all this from the visitors' area on the other side of the water. The kids felt as though Julius was a million miles away.

So far so good. Julius had been accepted, but he still had to meet Dennis, the "Big Boss," and that was really the most difficult and dangerous part. They decided to wait a little longer while Julius became used to his family.

"We've done it! We've done it!" said the adults. *They* felt they had succeeded. They knew this wasn't just Julius' day, but that he had made a step forward on behalf of chimpanzees all over the world. All chimpanzees are under threat and humans need to learn more and more about breeding them and caring for them.

"But is Julius going to stay here forever? Won't he visit us anymore?" asked Anne.

"He'll come once in a while. But you can see that he's become a chimpanzee among other chimpanzees."

The kids didn't think much of the success. To them this was a very sad day – they'd lost their best friend.

On the 12th of December Sanne had another unexpected baby. He was tiny, just like Julius had been. This explained why Sanne had so cruelly rejected Julius a second time – she couldn't cope, because she had another baby on the way. Julius now had a cute baby brother, named Kjell, after a kind zookeeper.

"Can we have Julius over for a Christmas and birthday party?" Siv pleaded one day when she saw Edvard and Marita baking a Christmas cake.

"No," replied Edvard firmly. "This year Julius will have to stay at the zoo."

But nothing was going to stop the kids at least bringing Julius a cake and some presents! So on the day after Christmas they all visited Julius. They put a tablecloth on the floor and all merrily munched cake.

Julius was the same as ever, full of fun and excitable, wanting to play with everyone.

The winter was dark and miserable. Edvard kept worrying. He knew Julius had to meet Dennis, the "Big Boss". If Dennis accepted him he'd truly be one of them.

But suddenly, to everyone's surprise, Dennis died of a heart attack. It was sad, but at least Julius wouldn't be hurt.

And now, who knows? Maybe after a few years Julius will become the big boss of the group. He's too good-natured now, but as the years go by he will become very large and much more like the other chimpanzees.

Spring again! Then glorious summer. Julius was famous now because of the T.V. show about him. Thousands of people came to the zoo, and everyone wanted to see him. He was a star! He was allowed off Monkey Island and ran around freely. He was a naughty chimp – every so often he would snatch a piece of cake from an unsuspecting person at the open-air restaurant.

Carl, Austen, Anne and Siv were his most special visitors.

One day Doctor Glad and Edvard sat talking, playing with the other monkeys, watching Julius.

"Julius seems to behave just like the other monkeys. But when he's with us humans, he's just like a little person," said Edvard.

"Yes, Julius knows a lot about people, but we know very little about him," said Doctor Glad. "The differences between humans and chimpanzees are not nearly as great as you would think. Julius does things that we do, but he does them in his own way. He's just completely himself and we could all learn a lot from him."

Then came the biggest breakthrough of all. Julius started to look after his nervous little brother, Kjell, lovingly reassuring him and hugging him whenever he needed it.

It seemed that the kindness Julius had been given had left a permanent good mark on him.

Julius was now given the responsibility of caring for his little brother by his family. And so he became fully accepted by the chimps. Little Kjell had good reason to look up to his brother.

At three years old, Julius weighed 33 pounds. He had weighed only three pounds at birth. A fully grown chimp can weigh 165 pounds and live to 50. For a few more years Julius can sometimes mix with people, but when he gets bigger and stronger he won't be allowed to anymore. Then he'll be just as strong as old Dennis was. Chimpanzees grow to be very strong, so strong humans don't dare get close to them.

In the cool autumn Marita and Julius sat quietly together. They sat this way for a long, long time.

They hugged and kissed each other fondly and in their own special way, they were saying goodbye.

"Mommy, do you think Julius will ever forget us?" asked Siv.

"No, I don't think so. Will you ever forget Julius?" asked Marita.

"No! He grew up with us and I love him. I'll always think of his birthday whenever everyone's celebrating Christmas and whenever there's joy everywhere."